Henry and Mudge
AND THE
Starry Night

The Seventeenth Book of Their Adventures

Story by Cynthia Rylant
Pictures by Suçie Stevenson

READY-TO-READ

ALADDIN PAPERBACKS

For Virginia Duncan, with many thanks—CR
For Travis and Grayson Voges—SS

THE HENRY AND MUDGE BOOKS

First Aladdin Paperbacks Edition May 1999

Aladdin Paperbacks
An imprint of Simon & Schuster
Children's Publishing Division
1230 Avenue of the Americas
New York, NY 10020

The text of this book was set in 18-point Goudy
The illustrations were rendered in pen-and-ink and watercolor

Printed and bound in the United States of America

30 29 28 27 26 25 24 23 22

The Library of Congress has cataloged the hardcover edition as follows:
Rylant, Cynthia.
    Henry and Mudge and the starry night : the seventeenth book of their adventures /
by Cynthia Rylant ; illustrated by Suçie Stevenson.
        p.   cm. — (The Henry and Mudge books)
    Summary: Henry, his big dog Mudge, and his parents go on a quiet camping trip to
Big Bear Lake, enjoying the clean smell of trees and wonderful green dreams.
    ISBN-13: 978-0-689-81175-3 (hc.)   ISBN-10: 0-689-81175-6 (hc.)
    [1. Dogs—Fiction. 2. Camping—Fiction.] I. Stevenson, Suçie, ill.
II. Title. III. Series: Rylant, Cynthia. Henry and Mudge books.
PZ7.R982Hear 1998
[E]—dc21 96-44443
ISBN-13: 978-0-689-82586-6 (pbk.)   ISBN-10: 0-689-82586-2 (pbk.)
0511 LAK

Contents

Big Bear Lake

In August
Henry and Henry's big dog Mudge
always went camping.
They went with Henry's parents.

Henry's mother had been
a Camp Fire Girl,
so she knew all about camping.
She knew how to set up a tent.

She knew how to build a campfire.

She knew how to cook camp food.

Henry's dad didn't know
anything about camping.
He just came with a guitar
and a smile.

Henry and Mudge loved camping.

This year they were going to

Big Bear Lake, and Henry

couldn't wait.

"We'll see deer, Mudge," Henry said.

Mudge wagged.

"We'll see raccoons," said Henry.

Mudge shook Henry's hand.

"We might even see
a *bear*," Henry said.

Henry was not so sure

he wanted to see a bear.

He shivered and put

an arm around Mudge.

Mudge gave a big, slow,
loud yawn.

He drooled on Henry's foot.

Henry giggled.

"No bear will get *us*, Mudge,"
Henry said.

"We're *too slippery!*"

A Good Smelly Hike

Henry and Mudge
and Henry's parents
drove to Big Bear Lake.
They parked the car
and got ready to hike.

17

Everyone had a backpack,

even Mudge.

(His had lots of crackers.)

Henry's mother said, "Let's go!"

And off they went.

They walked and walked
and climbed and climbed.
It was beautiful.

Henry saw a fish jump

straight out of a stream.

He saw a doe and her fawn.

He saw waterfalls
and a rainbow.

Mudge didn't see much of anything.

He was smelling.

Mudge loved to hike and smell.

He smelled a raccoon from yesterday.

He smelled a deer from last night.

He smelled an oatmeal cookie
from Henry's back pocket.
"Mudge!" Henry laughed,
giving Mudge the cookie.

Finally Henry's mother picked
a good place to camp.

Henry's parents set up the tent.

Henry unpacked the food and

pans and lanterns.

Mudge unpacked a ham sandwich.

Finally the camp was almost ready.

It needed just one more thing:

"Who knows the words to
'Love Me Tender'?"
said Henry's father with a smile,
pulling out his guitar.
Henry looked at Mudge
and groaned.

Green Dreams

It was a beautiful night.
Henry and Henry's parents
lay on their backs by the fire
and looked at the sky.

Henry didn't know
there were so many stars
in the sky.

"There's the Big Dipper,"
said Henry's mother.
"There's the Little Dipper,"
said Henry.

"There's E. T.,"
said Henry's dad.

Mudge wasn't looking at stars.

He was chewing on a log.

He couldn't get logs this good

at home.

Mudge loved camping.

Henry's father sang one more
sappy love song,
then everyone went
inside the tent to sleep.

Henry's father and mother snuggled.

Henry and Mudge snuggled.

It was as quiet as quiet could be.

Everyone slept safe and sound and

there were no bears, no scares.

Just the clean smell of trees . . .

and wonderful green dreams.